Every child learns to read in a different way and at his or her own speed. You can help your young reader improve and become more confident by encouraging his or her own interests and abilities. You can also guide your child's spiritual development by reading stories with biblical values and Bible stories, like I Can Read! books published by Zonderkidz. From books your child reads with you to the first books he or she reads alone, there are I Can Read! books for every stage of reading:

SHARED READING
Basic language, word repetition, and whimsical illustrations, ideal for sharing with your emergent reader.

BEGINNING READING
Short sentences, familiar words, and simple concepts for children eager to read on their own.

READING WITH HELP
Engaging stories, longer sentences, and language play for developing readers.

READING ALONE
Complex plots, challenging vocabulary, and high-interest topics for the independent reader.

ADVANCED READING
Short paragraphs, chapters, and exciting themes for the perfect bridge to chapter books.

I Can Read! books have introduced children to the joy of reading since 1957. Featuring award-winning authors and illustrators and a fabulous cast of beloved characters, I Can Read! books set the standard for beginning readers.

A lifetime of discovery begins with the magical words *"I Can Read!"*

Visit www.icanread.com for information on enriching your child's reading experience.
Visit www.zonderkidz.com for more Zonderkidz I Can Read! titles.

People look at the outward appearance, but the
Lord looks at the heart.
—1 Samuel 16:7

ZONDERKIDZ

The Princess Twins Play in the Garden
Copyright © 2011 by Mona Hodgson
Illustrations © 2015 byJulie Olson

Requests for information should be addressed to:
Zonderkidz, 3900 *Sparks Dr. SE, Grand Rapids, Michigan 49546*

This edition: ISBN 978-0-310-75050-5 (softcover)

This edition: ISBN 978-0-310-75313-1 (hardcover)

Library of Congress Cataloging-in-Publication Data

Hodgson, Mona Gansber, 1954–
    The princess twins play in the garden / Mona Hodgson.
        p. cm. – (I can read!)
    Summary: Twin princesses Abby and Emma thank God for a lovely day playing with their
    friends in the garden.
        ISBN 978-0-310-72705-7 (softcover)
    [1. Princesses—Fiction. 2. Twins—Fiction. 3. Sister—Fiction. 4. Christian life—Fiction.] I. Title
    PZ7.H6649Pvp 2012
    [E]—dc22   2010052447

All Scripture quotations, unless otherwise indicated, are taken from The Holy Bible, *New
International Version®, NIV®.* Copyright © 1973, 1978, 1984, 2011 by Biblica, Inc.® Used by
permission. All rights reserved worldwide.

Any Internet addresses (websites, blogs, etc.) and telephone numbers in this book are offered
as a resource. They are not intended in any way to be or imply an endorsement by Zondervan,
nor does Zondervan vouch for the content of these sites and numbers for the life of this book.

Zonderkidz is a trademark of Zondervan.

Editor: Mary Hassinger
Art direction & design: Jamie DeBruyn

Printed in China

15 16 17 18 19 20 /DHC/ 7 6 5 4 3 2 1

The Princess Twins Play in the Garden

Story by Mona Hodgson
Pictures by Julie Olson

4

Princess Emma and Princess Abby
walked in the castle garden.

"God made this a lovely day,"

Princess Abby said to her sister.

Emma stopped and screamed.

"There's a bug on my pretty dress."

"It will get my dress dirty.

Get it off me!" Emma said.

Abby gently lifted the ladybug

and set it on a rose.

"Thank you," said Emma.

Abby and Emma saw their friends.

"It's time for our playdate,"

said Abby.

Princess Abby ran down the hill.

Princess Emma walked down the hill.

She didn't want her dress

to get dirty.

She wanted to look pretty.

"Have fun at the castle,"
said Mrs. Lee.
She waved good-bye
to her children.

"Let's play in the garden,"
said Princess Abby.
The children ran up the hill
to the castle.

"We can have tea," said Emma.

"I don't want to get dirty."

The children had a tea party

in the garden.

Abby gave her friends rides
on her pony.

Emma sat in a chair and watched.

"A princess must look pretty,"
Emma said.

Abby and her friends

made sand castles.

The children played soccer

with Princess Abby.

A muddy ball hit Emma's dress.

"How could you?" she said

to her friend who'd kicked it.

Tears filled the girl's eyes.

"I'm sorry," she said.

Emma was sorry she'd yelled.

"That's okay," she said.

Emma hugged her friend.

"Let's play," said Emma.

She kicked the soccer ball.

Mrs. Lee waved.

It was time to go home.

Emma and Abby ran down the hill
with the children.

"Mama, we had lots of fun,"
said the children.

Mrs. Lee smiled at the princesses.

"Thank you," she said.

"You are both lovely girls."

A ladybug landed on Emma's dress.

She smiled and prayed,

"Thank you, God, for a lovely day."